HER SISTER'S LIE

Amish Romance

HANNAH MILLER

Tica House
Publishing

Sweet Romance that Delights and Enchants!

Personal Word from the Author

To My Dear Readers,

How exciting that you have chosen one of my books to read. Thank you! I am proud to now be part of the team of writers at Tica House Publishing who work joyfully to bring you stories of hope, faith, courage, and love.

Please feel free to contact me as I love to hear from my readers. I would like to personally invite you to sign up for updates and to become part of our **Exclusive Reader Club** —it's completely Free to join! Hope to see you there!

With love,

Hannah Miller

VISIT HERE to Join our Reader's Club and to Receive Tica House Updates:

https://amish.subscribemenow.com/

Chapter One

Snow drifted lazily downward, a threadbare carpet of white on the ground that hadn't been there when Dinah had entered the Potters' farmhouse for church that morning. Still, straggles of green stuck up through the white, a stubborn show that it was not so cold yet.

But whatever the weather, January always felt cold to Dinah. Post Christmas, with nothing to do but wait for the spring thaw to begin, Dinah couldn't help but feel blue. Preaching service helped—it was a welcome distraction. She knew that the cold months couldn't last forever, that the winter was *Gott*'s test. They would get through the dark and the cold and appreciate the warmer months all the more for it.

Dinah turned as she heard Aaron Burner's voice behind them.

Funny, how even when she was lost in her own thoughts, she was still finely attuned to that voice. She would recognize it even in the most crowded marketplace. But it was Claudia's name he was calling, not hers. Still, Dinah turned with her sister and smiled warmly at Aaron as he approached. His green-eyed gaze flicked to Dinah briefly before settling back on Claudia.

Aaron was a dark-haired, slim man, but Dinah had seen him working outdoors, and knew that muscle corded his arms and legs. He was stronger than he looked, that was for sure. Even now, in the deep of winter, his skin was dark and weathered from so much time spent outdoors. Dinah wasn't sure if it was even possible for Aaron to look pale the way she and Claudia did in these colder months.

"Aaron," Claudia said warmly, stepping toward him a little, leaving barely enough room to breathe. "How did you like the service?"

"Oh, well enough," Aaron said. "Although I find myself a little distracted of late. I think it must be the cold."

Claudia laughed, although Dinah wasn't sure what was so funny—she understood only too well how the icy, darker months toyed with the mind.

"Well, I'm sure we can find a way to warm you up," Claudia said, in a tone Dinah didn't much like.

Aaron's cheeks reddened a little, and he cast his eyes down at the whitening ground for a moment, but then he laughed. "You're too much, Claudia," he said, but there was only affection in his tone.

"So they tell me," Claudia said happily, then turned to Dinah, her look annoyed. "Are you really so cold, sister?"

Dinah realized then that she'd been shivering, and she tightened her cloak around her. "Yes," she said, a little embarrassed. She didn't want Aaron to think she was weak.

"Perhaps you should go and sit in the buggy, then."

Dinah wasn't sure what sitting in the open buggy would do for her, but she knew a dismissal when she heard one.

"I think I shall," she said. "*Gut* day, Aaron." She nodded to him before turning away toward the buggy waiting further down the driveway.

"I'd best be off as well," she heard Aaron say. "I think I'm starting to get the shivers now, too."

Dinah didn't hear Claudia's reply, her voice being too low to overhear, and maybe that was a good thing. Dinah didn't like the way Claudia spoke to Aaron, but she supposed that was just jealousy. Claudia and Aaron had been friends a long time, and Dinah had never really fit into that friendship. More recently, Claudia had admitted to their parents and to Dinah, that the two of them were courting.

Bitterness rose up her throat at the thought, but she pushed it back down again. Aaron was a good man, gentle and kind, hardworking, and yes, sometimes funny, and didn't Dinah want that for her sister? Of course, she did. Her own feelings for Aaron would fade, she supposed, over time. For now, it was merely another test, and one she did not mean to fail.

Down in the cellar, Dinah loaded a basket with all the things her mother had asked for—jars of pickled beetroot, pickled carrots, a few potatoes, and a butternut squash. Meanwhile, Claudia had gotten the slightly less desirable job of plucking and gutting the chicken. Although Dinah preferred her task in the cellar, she disliked this room. It was dark and musty, full of cobwebs and shadows, and it made her feel uneasy. The room smelled of dampness and slightly of vinegar. She gathered the supplies and hurried back up the stairs where daylight still lingered.

Claudia was standing over the large kitchen sink, muttering to herself as she pulled out the chicken's entrails. Dinah preferred not to look if she could help it. Her brothers had often laughed at her for it, but she hated killing the animals on their farm, and usually ate as little meat as possible.

In truth, Dinah never could understand how Claudia got away with doing the task in the kitchen instead of outside. But then, Claudia was good at getting her own way, something that Dinah wasn't too skilled at doing.

Dinah laid her basket on the kitchen counter, out of sight of the chicken in the sink, and unloaded it. She set the potatoes into a colander to wash when Claudia was finished and began the arduous task of peeling and cutting up the squash.

"It was nice to see Aaron today," Dinah said, making conversation. She hated to work in absolute silence. "He looks quite well, don't you think?"

Claudia chuckled, a low sound, as though at some private joke. "Aaron's a sweetheart," she said. "It's always right nice to see him."

"Have you been out riding with him recently?" Dinah asked. It had been a while since she and Claudia had talked in this manner, and although the subject often pained Dinah, she still wanted to know what was going on in his sister's life.

"Oh, not this week," Claudia said, but she didn't sound bothered about it. "In fact..." She glanced around, perhaps making sure their mother hadn't re-entered the room. "I suppose I should make a confession."

Dinah stilled her knife. "Oh?"

"I've met someone else."

Dinah's heart clenched. She felt strange, a little light-headed, perhaps. Confusion and disbelief clouded her thoughts.

Claudia was seeing someone else now? Why would she choose another man over Aaron? How could *anyone* choose another man over Aaron?

"You have to promise not to tell another soul," Claudia said, her gaze locking on Dinah's.

Slowly, Dinah nodded.

"His name's Gary. Ach, but he's just so *handsome*. I mean, have you ever had that whole-body shiver when just looking at a person? It feels really *gut*. In truth, it's a delicious feeling."

A delicious feeling? Dinah frowned. That was a mighty odd way of wording it. But her cheeks grew warm—wasn't that how she felt when she saw Aaron? Though she would never admit it out loud. Besides, she wasn't sure she wanted to know so much about Claudia's body shivers.

"So... you're not courting Aaron anymore?" she asked, keeping her voice quiet in case anyone was near the kitchen door.

Claudia shook her head. "I never was," she said casually. "I mean, like I said, Aaron's a dear, but I just don't think of him that way. I have other plans."

Dinah set down her knife on the chopping block, frowning. "So, you lied?"

"I didn't mean to lie to *you*, only to *Mamm* and *Dat*. They wouldn't approve of me and Gary." She laughed, a tinkling sound filling the room. "*Nee*, they wouldn't approve at all. "And that is why you must not to tell a soul."

Dinah's frown deepened. Who was this Gary person? Dinah was sure there was no one by that name in their district. Was he from out of town? A Mennonite, maybe?

"Why wouldn't they approve?" she asked slowly, fearing her sister's answer.

"Well, for one, he's *Englisch*."

"*Englisch?*" Dinah exclaimed, far too loudly, and then quickly lowered her voice. "What on earth are you doing with an *Englischer*? Are you crazy? *Ach,* but what would *Dat* say?"

Claudia smirked. "What am I *not* doing with him, is more the question." She laughed, as though she hadn't just set a ticking bomb down on the kitchen counter.

"But... but Claudia. You can't be dating an *Englischer*. You must be telling me another lie," Dinah hissed, but that wasn't quite true. Unfortunately, she believed every word Claudia was saying. It would be just like her rebellious sister to do such a thing.

"Come now, Dinah. You can't tell me you don't understand. Are you saying that there's *no one* you'd risk everything for? Surely, there's someone in your life? You're of age."

"But this isn't about me," Dinah snapped. Even if she'd wanted to answer her sister, she knew the answer was no.

Even for Aaron, she wouldn't risk her family, her friends, her relationship with *Gott* and the church. She was fond of Aaron —maybe even more than fond of him, and yes, she secretly wanted him to court her, but there were some things that were more important. Didn't Claudia understand that?

"You're unhappy with me," Claudia said, and she sounded sad, now. "I thought you might be at least a little excited."

"*Excited?* By what? At the prospect of you leaving us? At the idea that I might never see my sister again? The idea that this could completely break apart our family? *Ach,* Claudia, you can't be serious."

Claudia shrugged but was quiet for a moment. "It doesn't have to break apart our family," she said then, and Dinah wondered how she could be so deluded. "You won't tell anyone, right? You did promise. If no one finds out, then there won't be a problem."

Dinah shook her head, still trying to grasp what Claudia was saying. There had been other times in the past when Claudia had done something which had disturbed Dinah. Other times when Dinah had been forced to keep a secret because of a promise she'd made in haste to her sister. But this time? This time was gravely serious.

She was torn between the promise she'd just made and her duty to the rest of her family. But maybe this thing with 'Gary' would resolve itself. Claudia had always been rather impulsive. Perhaps this was just something she needed to get out of her system, and in time, she'd realize it was all a big mistake. If that were the case, there was no sense in telling everyone about it. It would only hurt them, the way it was hurting Dinah now.

No, it was better they not know, at least for now.

"*Nee*," she said reluctantly. "I won't tell."

Chapter Two

The wheels of the buggy rumbled over the unsealed road, the horse pulling it along at a sedate pace. Aaron didn't mind. Lily was getting old, and he was in no hurry. It was likely they would have to retire her in a year or two, and he would have to find a good place for her to spend that retirement. He knew father wouldn't want to keep her once she was no longer useful, but he was sure he could persuade him to let her go somewhere nice. It wouldn't cost them anything, after all, and Lily had earned a few peaceful last years.

He spotted a figure walking at the side of the road in the distance, and only when the buggy was side by side with the woman did he realize it was Claudia Baer's sister, Dinah. He stopped the buggy and bid her good morning. Dinah glanced up at him, and he was struck by the deep blue color of her eyes. She wished him a good morning in response.

"Are you heading to town?" he asked, and she nodded. "Why not hop in then? I'll save you the time."

She looked at him, biting her lip. As far as he could see, it should be an easy decision to make—walk the four miles into town or catch a lift and get there in less than half the time—but she seemed to agonize over it for a moment. Eventually, she agreed, and he reached down to help her climb up. Her hand was cool, her grip firm. When she was settled, she turned to him and smiled.

"Thank you," she said. "It's right cold this morning, and I appreciate it."

"You're more than welcome," he replied.

They rode together in silence for a while, Dinah never quite taking up the conversation starters Aaron dropped here and there. She'd always been a quiet sort of person, he supposed. Perhaps, it was because her sister was always so loud, and Dinah rarely had a chance to get a word in. That, or she just didn't like him very much, and preferred not to speak much with him. That thought stung a little, and he hoped it wasn't true.

"Where in town are you headed?"

"The fabric shop. The one on the east side of town."

"Ah. Keeping busy, then?"

"Always," Dinah said with a small smile.

"Well, I'll drop you off at the end of the street, then. And if you like, I can pick you up from there in about an hour or so."

"Oh, that's all right," Dinah told him, a little too quickly. "I don't mind the walk, and I wouldn't want to trouble you."

"Dinah," he said, turning to look at her squarely. "It ain't too much trouble. What would be more trouble, is me knowing you were walking all this way in the cold."

He smiled at the way her cheeks became tinged with pink. She cast her gaze down into her lap at her hands clasped together.

"All right, then," she said, so quietly he struggled to hear. "Thank you."

Aaron returned to the fabric shop a little over an hour after he'd dropped Dinah off, expecting to see her there, waiting. But when he got there, she was nowhere to be found. He frowned. Had she given up on him? But no, there she was, hurrying toward him, her basket swinging from the crook of her arm.

When she reached him, she seemed a little breathless. "I'm so sorry," she said, her words blurring together. "I lost track of time. Have you been waiting long for me? I do hope not."

"*Ach,* but I've been waiting for ages," he teased.

"Oh *nee!* I'm so sorry." She appeared crestfallen, her mouth an unhappy curve.

"I was joking," he admitted sheepishly, never thinking she would take him seriously. "I only just got here."

She frowned, but he thought he detected a bit of amusement there, too. So, she did have a sense of humor, after all.

"I'm glad you didn't wait long," she said, her voice serious. "Are you ready to leave then?"

"If you like," Aaron said, wondering why he'd felt so free to tease her. They didn't know each other that well, did they? He hoped he hadn't annoyed her, and he suddenly wanted to make sure he hadn't. Perhaps, he could do something unexpected and nice.

"I would like to make one stop first," he told her.

He drove the buggy out of town, with Dinah sitting primly beside him.

"You like bird watching, *ain't so?*" he asked. He was sure Claudia had told him that once, but he might have misremembered.

"Oh, *jah*," Dinah said. "Did Claudia tell you? We have a falcon's nest in a tree in our yard."

He shook his head. "She didn't tell me about that, *nee*."

"*Ach, jah...* Well, Claudia doesn't appreciate it as much as I do, I suppose."

"I doubt your Claudia has much patience to sit and watch for birds all day."

Dinah giggled, then, the first laugh Aaron had gotten out of her all day. "*Nee,* she doesn't. Not that I have time to watch them all day. Although I wish I did."

He hesitated a moment, for he didn't want to drag Dinah away from anything important. His idea *was* a little frivolous.

"Do you have the time for one stop?" he asked. "It won't take long, and I think you'll appreciate it."

Dinah nodded. "You've saved me a *gut* amount of time by driving me," she said. "And you've got me intrigued now, so I have to ask. Where are we going?"

Aaron just smiled. "You'll see," he said.

Chapter Three

Dinah had never really spent all that much time with Aaron before, and never alone. It should have been nice, she thought, and a little exciting to be with him now, but instead guilt clawed at her insides. He was being so nice. And in return, Dinah was helping her sister lie about him. She was sure Aaron didn't know about the mistruth Claudia hold told their parents, and she knew he had a right to that information. But she'd promised Claudia she wouldn't say anything to anyone, and that included Aaron.

Aaron pulled the buggy to the left, and they drove through the park gates, beneath the rows of barren trees. Dinah wondered what they were doing there, but she kept still. She would see soon enough.

Aaron parked the buggy close to the pond, tying the horse to a leafless tree. He patted the horse's flank before leading Dinah toward the pond. The water was half-frozen, and she had the fleeting thought that she hoped none of the children in their district would try to walk on it. More than one drowning had occurred in such a way.

She took a deep breath, the cold air sinking into her lungs. It was nice, she thought, to be here with Aaron by her side while it was so still and peaceful. This was the kind of moment she had so often thought about, the kind of moment she had been sure would never happen. Even if they were only here as friends, pleasure bubbled inside her.

At the edge of the pond, Aaron stopped. He was quiet for a moment, his gaze scanning the area around them. Then he pointed. "Look," he said.

Dinah looked. For a moment she didn't see anything, but then Aaron pointed again, and Dinah followed his finger to the other side of the pond. She saw them, then. Two fluffy downy woodpeckers flitting about in the trees. They moved quickly, before landing on the trunks.

"So beautiful," Dinah exclaimed. And they were, not just the woodpeckers, but also this moment, standing at the water's edge with Aaron beside her, the ground crisp under their feet.

They stayed but a minute or two longer, lingering in the calm beauty of the lake and the birds. Dinah found herself not wanting to leave—wanting to stretch this moment forever. How she loved being with Aaron like this. But Aaron seemed concerned about getting her back home. "Shall we go?" he asked.

She nodded, albeit reluctantly, and followed him back to the buggy.

Later, Aaron dropped Dinah off outside her home, and Dinah waved him goodbye. She felt like something had changed between them that day. They were no longer only connected by Claudia. Instead, they were friends in their own right. At least, they would be, if Dinah wasn't keeping such a terrible secret from him. How could they be friends, really, if Dinah was lying to him? Would he ever find out what Claudia had claimed? Would he ever find out that Dinah knew about it? And what then?

He would dislike her for sure.

All the joy that had filled her only moments before leaked out of her, and as she trudged up the frosty driveway, her breath steaming in the air, she knew her affection toward him was futile.

She found her mother in the front room, and they sat for a while, mending clothes. Claudia wasn't in, *Mamm* said. She'd gone out for the day, with Aaron. Dinah bit her lip, and her guilt soared. Claudia wasn't with Aaron, she knew, but was probably with Gary.

Please. Let Gott *show you the light, dear sister. I don't want to be without you. I don't want this* Englischer *to take you away from us.*

Dinah breakfasted early the next morning, taking her meal alone before anyone else was up. Claudia was usually the earliest riser, but perhaps she was sleeping in after being out all day. Dinah hadn't seen her before she'd gone to bed the night before, for she'd been tired and had headed to her room a little early.

She would have to make more of an effort with Claudia, she decided. Perhaps, just by being a better sister, she could persuade Claudia that some things were more important than her fantasy with Gary. Things like family. And God.

She would talk to Claudia later, she decided. Give her time to wake up, and then perhaps they could talk together while doing their chores. Perhaps it was possible, somehow, to learn Claudia's motivation, to understand why she would do something like this. Then, maybe Dinah could figure out a way to dissuade her.

Dinah wasn't about to sit around all morning waiting for her sister, though. Once she had eaten her eggs and drunk her tea, she donned her cloak and headed outside to begin feeding the cows and chickens.

As always, her favorite cow, Penny, lumbered up to the fence and nuzzled her head against Dinah's shoulder, nearly pushing her backward. Penny's long, rough tongue licked at Dinah's cloak, and Dinah laughed, the weight of worry dropping from her shoulders, at least for a moment. She cut the twine from the first bale of hay and began pulling it into clumps and throwing it over the fence. Soon all six cows were crowded around, eager to feed.

Dinah watched them for a while. Once winter passed, it would be calving season, and some of these ladies would have little ones to nurse. She always liked that time of year, although taking the calves away a few weeks later was sometimes hard. Some, though, would be reunited. They usually kept one or two of the female calves each year. Some would go to neighboring farms, and others would be sold at auction. Dinah had a hard time not getting too attached. Claudia was better at that, she knew. Claudia enjoyed the calves well enough, but once they began to grow, her interest flagged.

Dinah said goodbye to the cows and headed back inside, expecting Claudia to be in the kitchen, but she wasn't. *Mamm* was cooking eggs while *Dat* sat at the table, drinking a cup of tea.

"*Ach*, you are up," he said, glancing at her. "I was beginning to think I'd produced two lazy daughters."

Dinah frowned at him. "I've already eaten, and I've never been one to be lazy. I hope you know that, *Dat*."

He chuckled. "Of course not. I'm just teasing you. I don't think I've ever known you to be lazy. Not even when you're under the weather. Claudia, on the other hand..."

"Claudia can afford to be lazy from time to time," Dinah told him, taking a seat at the table. "Since she always seems to manage twice as much when she's working."

"*Jah,* she can be a whirlwind, that one," *Dat* agreed.

"Speaking of Claudia," *Mamm* said, setting a large platter of eggs on the table. "I'd better go and wake her. She won't want to miss out on breakfast. Dinah, dear, could you finish the toast?"

Dinah did as she was asked and set the only slightly burnt toast on the table beside the butter dish.

Mamm came back down, her lips set in a thin line, her voice stern to mask the worry in her eyes. "Dinah, dear, did you see your sister this morning at all?"

Dinah shook her head. "*Nee,* I haven't. Like I said, I ate a bite and then went out to tend the animals."

Mamm's frown only deepened. "She must have gotten up early, then. Was she outside with you? *Nee, nee,* you said you haven't seen her. It's not like her to make her bed first thing. She usually has breakfast and helps *red* up the kitchen first. Why? I don't know, but that's always been her habit. Did you see her last night at all?"

"*Nee,*" Dinah said slowly, worry beginning to sizzle inside her. "I went to bed early. I didn't see her come in."

"You don't think..." *Mamm's* gaze flicked from Dinah to *Dat*. "*Nee*, I'm sure it's fine."

"Where was she yesterday?" *Dat* said, his back straightening, his tea abandoned.

"She was out with Aaron Burner," *Mamm* told him. "But I can't believe that Aaron— I mean, you don't think?"

Guilt twisted Dinah's stomach. She knew only too well that this had nothing to do with Aaron. But if Dinah hadn't come home last night, then that meant... Dinah didn't even want to think it.

"I don't believe we should jump to conclusions," *Dat* said after a long moment. "We'll give her an hour. She might have gone out for an early morning walk. But after that, we'll have to go looking. There's a snowstorm expected to come in from the north this evening. I don't want her out in that."

Chapter Four

Claudia didn't come back in the hour that followed. Dinah had known all along that she wouldn't, but something in her had still hoped. She'd been sent to fetch her brothers from their farms down the road for a family meeting. While everyone talked, discussing all the possible places Claudia might have gone, Dinah said nothing, torn between telling her family the truth and betraying her sister's confidence.

Finally, Jonathan and Noah were sent out to look for Claudia. They weren't happy about it. It was bitterly cold outside, and they both had properties and families of their own to look out for, especially with a snowstorm likely due that evening. They didn't seem to think Claudia was in any danger, either. They knew her, and thought she'd likely run off with Aaron, although for *him*, it would be a little out of character, they admitted.

Dinah knew she couldn't let Aaron be blamed for Claudia's disappearance. The room quieter now. Dinah opened her mouth, ready to spill everything to her mother.

Then *Dat* returned, his heavy coat fastened up to his neck.

"This is ridiculous," he said. "I didn't want to insult the Burners if I can help it, but I'm sure now that young Aaron has a lot to answer for. You two stay here, in case Claudia comes home."

Dinah's eyes widened. He couldn't go to Aaron's family and start accusing Aaron of things. She scrambled up, grabbing her cloak from its peg as she hurried after her father out the door.

"Wait!" she cried, but he clearly didn't hear her.

She scrambled into the buggy after him, but he barely even seemed to notice her. She had to tell the truth now, before it was too late, but the words seemed stuck in her throat. She thought of Aaron and how much she liked him.

"*Dat*," she finally managed to spit out. "Claudia—"

"Whatever excuses you've conjured up for her, I don't want to hear them," he snapped.

"But, *Dat*, this ain't—"

"I mean it, daughter. I don't want to hear them. I know you've covered for Claudia before. But that stops now, do you hear? I don't want you to say—"

"But, *Dat!*"

"Dinah. Keep still. I'll handle this."

And then they were at the Burners' place. Dinah followed behind her father, miserably. It was too late, now. What had she allowed by not speaking up?

Although she couldn't see it from her place standing behind him, Dinah could imagine only too well the look on her father's face when Aaron opened the door to them. But then Aaron glanced behind her father, to her, and she could easily see his confusion. Dinah could taste blood—she'd been biting her lip again but hadn't realized she was breaking the skin.

"Is everything all right?" Aaron asked, concern lacing his words.

"Where's my daughter?" *Dat* demanded. "Where's Claudia? She never came home last night. She must have been with you. Is she here?"

Aaron's frown only deepened. "Here? *Nee*, she's not. Why would you think Claudia would be here?"

"Don't be coy with me, boy," *Dat* said.

"Coy?" Arron's voice was thick with dismay.

"I know what's going on. You're the one courting her," *Dat* snapped, and Dinah wanted to sink through the porch and into the ground. "You're the only one she would have run off with like that, so don't try to tell me—"

Aaron held up a hand, cutting *Dat* off mid-sentence. "Wait. Hold on a minute. I don't know where you've gotten this idea from, but I'm *not* courting Claudia."

"Don't lie to me! Claudia told us everything weeks ago, so don't think it's a secret."

"Mr. Baer, I can assure you, I'm *not* courting your daughter."

It was admirable, really, how controlled Aaron sounded in the face of *Dat*'s wrath. How reasonable he seemed. He acted as though he wasn't fazed, but Dinah knew he must be reeling inside with questions. Dinah was the only one who knew the truth here. She had to—

Dat turned to glare at her. "Dinah? Do you know anything about this?" he asked, his voice level again, but hard as stone.

"I—" She took a deep breath, her gaze focused on the wide boards beneath her feet. "Claudia lied. She was never courting Aaron. He doesn't have anything to do with this. He's just her friend."

Once she'd started, everything rushed out, a torrent of words all jumbling together. For a moment, both her father and Aaron were silent, and she wondered if they'd heard her properly.

It was Aaron who spoke first, not *Dat*. Dinah should have been grateful she wasn't being shouted at, but Aaron's voice made her feel even more guilty. "Dinah? Do you know where Claudia is now?"

Dinah shook her head. "I don't know where she is. But she said she was being courted by someone else. He's—" She took a deep, trembling breath. "He's an *Englischer*. She said his name was Gary. That's really all I know."

Dat stiffened but remained silent, and somehow that was worse than his shouting.

"All right," Aaron said after a moment. "You don't know anything else?"

Dinah shook her head again. She couldn't meet Aaron's eye. "I'm sorry," she mumbled.

"I'll help you look," Aaron offered. "I know my father will, too."

Dat was still glaring at Dinah. Her throat went dry, and she felt a deep quaking inside.

"An *Englischer?*" Dat said, his voice returning with a controlled growl. It was worse than if he'd blasted the words at her.

"*Jah*," Dinah muttered. "I'm sorry. I don't know who he is. Truly, I don't."

"An *Englischer?*" Dat repeated, but this time his voice cracked, and the horror and sadness in his tone were like a blow to Dinah.

Dinah hung her head. "*Jah, Dat.*"

"We'll help look," Aaron said, his voice gentle yet firm.

Dat blinked and looked momentarily lost. "*Jah. Jah.* Fine. *Gut.* We need to look for her. *Jah.*"

"I'll go get my father," Aaron said simply.

"Thank you," *Dat* said. He gave Aaron a desperate look. "But maybe... maybe you could keep the er... more sensitive details quiet?"

"Of course," Aaron said immediately. "I won't say a word."

Another lie, albeit a lie by omission, told on Claudia's behalf, Dinah thought bitterly.

She followed her father back to the buggy. Once seated, he turned to look at her. "You let me make a fool of myself here," he told her, disappointment and censure heavy in his words. "How long have you known about this?"

"Not long," Dinah told him. "A week or so."

"And you didn't think to tell us?"

Dinah hung her head again. "I hoped she'd change her mind. I didn't want to hurt everyone."

"You didn't want to hurt us?" His tone was incredulous. "We could have put a stop to this before it went any further, and now? Now your sister is *missing*. Do you think *that's* not hurting us?"

Dinah could only shake her head. Tears sprang hot from the corners of her eyes, and the world around her blurred. Why had she lied for Claudia? Why had Claudia asked that of her? Her father was right to be disappointed in her. She'd let everyone down, even Claudia.

And Aaron... now Aaron knew the truth of it, that Claudia had lied about him, and that Dinah had helped her to keep the lie.

She didn't stop crying the whole way home.

Chapter Five

Over the next couple of weeks, Dinah found that trust was a hard thing to win back once it had been lost. She'd always been the good daughter, the one everyone could rely on. Now her parents barely trusted her to go to the store for them anymore. She was chaperoned by one or the other of her brothers if not directly by her parents, and she'd seen several times a look of distrust in her mother's and father's eyes. It was as though she knew more than she'd told them, as though they believed she knew exactly where Claudia was and wouldn't tell them.

But she didn't. She didn't know anything and it sickened her with worry.

Her mother was barely speaking to her, and Jonathan, the

younger of her two older brothers, had asked her three times now if she knew anything more.

She busied herself with work in the yard just to get out of the house, despite the bitter cold and the regular flurries of snow. She mended fence panels alone, cleaned out the chicken coop more than was necessary, and shoveled up every last bit of cow and horse manure she could find. When she had to be inside, she would find herself sitting alone to darn or knit. Her mother often left the room when Dinah entered, as though she couldn't bear to be near her. It was as though Dinah was the one who'd abandoned them, not Claudia.

Dinah realized they were taking out the anger and hurt they felt over Claudia's betrayal on her, because Claudia wasn't there to receive it. Or maybe, it was just that Dinah had let them down, and they didn't yet know how to deal with her. Either way, Dinah needed to give them time and to spend that time proving she *was* a good daughter, that she *could* be trusted. Hopefully then, things would improve, but it was hard.

Adding to her sorrow, she had to deal with it all alone. The only person she could have talked to about this was Claudia, but of course, Claudia was no longer there. Dinah held out hope that she would return, and although that hope was receding daily, she felt there was still a slim chance that Claudia would realize she'd made a mistake. She could still come back.

Mother told curious folks that Claudia was visiting relatives at their horse farm in Illinois, but that wasn't going to hold things together for much longer. If Claudia was going to come back with any part of her reputation still intact, she needed to do it soon. The fact that her parents were lying to deal with the crisis didn't escape Dinah's attention, but she hardly thought it appropriate to mention. Instead, she kept to herself, her sorrow growing each day.

Sometimes, at a youth singing or after preaching service—and once at the feed store—Dinah ran into Aaron. She could barely meet his eyes anymore. She knew he must be angry with her, and disappointed, just like the rest of her family. Maybe even worse. Her heart sank when she saw him now. How could there be any hope of a relationship with him, after this? But still, he sometimes smiled at her, and she grasped onto those smiles, holding them close to her heart. But reality told her to quit dreaming. He was just being polite and keeping up appearances. She couldn't delude herself.

All her hope was used up wishing Claudia would come home.

Aaron had ticked just about everything off his mental list for the morning. He'd purchased everything his family needed—a new hammer, nails and screws, and some fencing wire, as well as a knife sharpener for the kitchen. He'd also picked up a new set of gloves for his mother. Her hands had been aching with the cold, and she'd been unable to keep up with tasks about the house. He wasn't sure how much the gloves would help, but it was the least he could offer her until the spring came. Until then, he and his sister Beth would have to do extra around the house.

He was ready to get back in his buggy and head home from town when he saw Dinah Baer out of the corner of his eye. He turned. She was coming out of the kitchen and homeware shop he'd been in just twenty minutes earlier. Perhaps he should leave without greeting her. She had barely looked his way since the incident at his family's home weeks ago. She undoubtedly didn't want to see him.

But, ignoring his own best advice, he headed toward her. She turned to see him at the last second, surprise crossing her face before her features smoothed out, shuttering down.

"*Gut* day, Dinah," he greeted her, touching the brim of his felt hat.

She nodded to him. "*Gut* day," she said, her tone sounding forcibly polite.

"How are things with you?" he asked. He knew she must be having a hard time with Claudia leaving the way she had. Whenever he saw Dinah now, she always looked so sad. He hadn't really had the time to talk with her properly, but now was as good a moment as any.

"They're all right, thank you," she said, and he knew that

wasn't true by the fact that she didn't quite meet his eye as she said it. "Spring will be here before we know it."

He nodded. He liked to think that spring would be upon them in no time at all, but it wasn't likely. Spring came late in Indiana. In any case, he hoped they would get some relief from the cold snap soon.

He took a deep breath. "Look, Dinah—"

He stopped as Mrs. Baer emerged from the store. She looked at him, then at her daughter, then back to him. He noted a slight look of mistrust in her eyes, but he couldn't tell whether it was for him or for Dinah. He certainly could think of nothing *he* had done to earn that look.

When she spoke, however, she sounded perfectly pleasant. "Aaron, how nice to see you. How's your *mamm?*"

"She's well enough," he told her. "A little trouble with the arthritis, but Beth and I are forcing her to take things a little easier for a while."

Mrs. Baer smiled and chuckled lightly. "I'm sure she appreciates that."

"Not in the slightest," he said with a grin, and just like that, the mistrustful look on her face vanished. "I'd best be getting on," he said, not wanting to linger and not wanting to risk the subject of Claudia coming up. He knew well enough that it was a sore topic. "But I'm sure I'll see you at preaching service come Sunday if not before."

The two women bid him good day and he took his leave, heading back to the buggy. As he walked, he couldn't help but reflect on the miserable look in Dinah's blue eyes. He remembered that she often seemed unhappy this time of year, possibly something to do with the weather, but this went deeper.

She must miss her sister terribly, he thought. He too, missed Claudia. They'd been friends, and he still didn't understand why she had lied about him like that. It hurt. And it hurt that Dinah had covered up for that lie, too. He'd liked Dinah, still did, and he sometimes fancied there might be something between them. But now...

He sighed, and gathered the buggy's reins in his gloved hands, before starting for home.

Chapter Six

Dinah thought maybe the cold snap was beginning to ease up a little. It had been a few days since the last snow, and she could see the ground again through the thin, patchy blanket of white. She'd done all her chores for the morning and decided to take time for a walk. She'd not gone far, just down to the creek and back, but the sun was nearing its midway point when she returned. She tipped her face up to it, hoping to gather a little of its warmth.

There was someone on their porch, she realized as she approached the house. The person was sitting on the lower step, hunched over, face in her hands. Dinah's heart began to beat quickly, and her jaw dropped. It was *Claudia*. Claudia had *come home*.

She wanted to shriek, to run to her sister and embrace her

fiercely. Instead, she kept to her slow pace, her heart still beating wildly in her chest. She stopped in front of her sister, looking down at her as Claudia looked up.

Claudia's eyes were red, dark shadows beneath them. Her nails, Dinah noticed as she unfurled her hands, were bitten to the quick. She had painted them, the way *Englischers* sometimes did, but that pale pink paint was chipping and peeling. *She looks terrible,* Dinah thought.

Dinah crouched, making them the same height, and forced a smile she hoped was welcoming. Claudia let out a sob and flung her arms around Dinah. Dinah didn't move for a moment, still stunned, but then she wrapped her arms around her sister, and held her while she cried.

After a few moments, the door opened. Dinah felt her mother's presence, but no words were spoken. After a while, Claudia leaned back and rubbed her eyes, sniffing loudly. Dinah stood and offered Claudia her hand. Their mother said nothing, only stepped aside to let the two young women through the door and into the house.

"I made a mistake," Claudia told their mother at the kitchen table. "A *big* mistake. I'm so sorry."

They were the words Dinah had most wanted to hear, but somehow, they felt hollow, not enough. Claudia had dumped a big mess over all their heads, and now that she was back, she would have to help clean that mess up before they could all move on.

Mamm made a big kettle of hot tea, but she didn't sit with them to drink it. The kitchen was quiet except for her clatter as she sliced bread and cold meats and opened jars of pickled eggs and beetroot.

Dinah was glad her sister was back, she really was, but one thought kept playing on her mind. *What now?* Where did they go from here?

The rest of the day was caught up with family, with their brothers exclaiming and shouting at Claudia, with *Dat* glowering but not speaking, with *Mamm* eventually bursting into tears and embracing her elder daughter tightly. It was too much for Dinah. She retreated to her room and shut the door.

It was only much later that she heard a soft knock on the wood. Claudia entered the room. "Dinah?" she called through the gloom, before crossing the floor to the small lantern on the bedside table and lighting it.

She sat on the end of Dinah's bed, her weight pulling at the quilts around Dinah's feet. "You're angry with me," she said, in a small voice.

"*Jah,*" Dinah said. "I am." There was no point sugar-coating it or pretend otherwise. She was done lying for Dinah, whether it was covering up for her or fibbing to make her feel better.

"I didn't mean to hurt you," Claudia said. "I... Well, I got carried away with Gary, I suppose. I thought I loved him."

"And now you don't?"

"Now, I don't know what I think." A small sob escaped her. "He's left me. I thought he was this great fellow, so romantic, you know? But then he just... I don't know. I'm so confused. One day he loved me, and I'm the greatest thing in his life, and the next, I'm nothing."

Dinah frowned. She couldn't help but feel sympathy for her sister, and anger at this man who had played with Claudia's heart, convincing her to run away from her church and her family, only to dump her weeks later. What sort of man behaved like that? And how had Claudia fallen for him in the first place?

"Everyone's so angry with me now. *Dat* won't even speak to me."

"They wouldn't speak to me for a few days, either," Dinah told her. "Once they found out I'd lied for you, they stopped trusting me. If you want that trust back, you'll have to earn it."

Claudia hung her head. "It shouldn't have to be this hard," she said softly.

"It's only this hard because you made it this hard," Dinah retorted. Had Claudia really expected to come back after everything that had happened and just go right back to the way things were before?

"I know. I'm sorry. I hope... I hope that at least *you* can forgive me. You're the only one I can really confide in."

Dinah frowned. "Of course, I can forgive you. I have to, don't I? It's what we believe," she said. "It might just... take a little time, that's all."

"I understand," Claudia said and stood. She smoothed down her skirt. "I'll leave you alone for now. See you in the morning, sister."

Dinah nodded. "See you in the morning."

It was Aaron's younger sister, Beth, who first told him that Claudia was back. The words came out of her mouth so casually. Evidently, she'd seen Claudia at the market, back from visiting family in Illinois, she said. Of course, Aaron knew the truth of it.

He left half his dinner untouched and went straight out to the buggy. Maybe he should give them some time, but if Claudia had been at the market, then perhaps she'd already been back for a few days, and he needed to talk to her. He'd spent weeks wondering what had happened—what had caused her to use him in her lie. He almost understood her running off with an *Englischer*—she'd always been a little wild like that—but using him as her cover story, lying about him... *that* he didn't understand. And, if he were honest, there was still a big part of him that was worried for her. How was she? Had she come through this all right?

It was Dinah he saw first. She was coming out of the shed as he drove up, and he slowed the buggy to a stop in front of her.

"It's true?" he asked. "She's back?"

Dinah nodded her head.

"Is she..." the words caught in his throat. "Is she all right?"

"She's fine," Dinah said. "Still the same Claudia." Her mouth was a thin line, though, and bitterness tinged her voice. She must still be angry with her sister, and Aaron couldn't blame her for that.

"I'd like to speak with her," he said, and Dinah nodded again before escorting him up to the house.

They sat together in the front room, he and Claudia, while Dinah let them be. Silence stretched between them. Eventually, Aaron cleared his throat.

"Why did you tell your parents we were courting?" he asked. "Why did you lie, when you could have just said nothing at all?"

Claudia shrugged. "I needed something to say. Some excuse for my absences in the evenings. And since we spent time together already, you were the obvious choice. I'm sorry. I know I treated you badly, and I shouldn't have used you like that." Tears sprang from her eyes, and Aaron's heart twisted in his chest. "I suppose you know the truth?"

"A little," he admitted. "I know you went off with some *Englischer*."

"I got so caught up in myself, in *him*, I couldn't even think about anyone else. I thought he loved me, but I was wrong. So so wrong. He left me. Why am I like this, Aaron? I never think about the consequences, do I? I just *act*, and usually like a complete fool. I'm always sorry afterward." She sighed. "Sometimes I wish I was more like Dinah. She's so *sensible*."

Aaron nodded. Dinah had a solid head on her shoulders, he could tell that. She was down-to-earth and didn't get carried away with flights of fancy the way her sister did. In many ways, the two sisters were total opposites of each other. It was a wonder they seemed so close. Although whether they were as close as all that now, Aaron didn't know. He knew that Claudia leaving like she had hurt Dinah deeply. He had seen it written all over Dinah's face when she'd answered the door to him moments ago.

"Maybe you could learn a few things from her," he told Claudia, not unkindly, as she scrubbed the tears from her face with the heel of her hand. "You hurt her, you know. You hurt everyone. Me included."

"I know. I'm sorry."

"But you know why you hurt them so much, don't you?"

She shook her head but still answered. "Because I embarrassed them."

"*Nee*, because they *love* you. They care about you, your life, your soul."

Claudia sighed. "You, too?" she asked.

"You're my friend," he told her. "Of course, I care about you."

She nodded then and forced a smile.

"And I don't know who this Gary fellow is, but he was a fool to have left you."

"You always know how to make me feel better," she said, sniffing.

Aaron smiled, glad to have eased a little of the pain in her heart.

Chapter Seven

Dinah was glad to have her sister back, she was. But it was strange, seeing Claudia at the breakfast table as though nothing had happened. In their parents' eyes, Dinah was once again the loving daughter, and even though she was a year younger than Claudia, Dinah was now often nominated as Claudia's chaperone when everyone else was too busy. Dinah wondered at that. She had lied for Claudia before, after all, how did they know she wouldn't do it again?

She told herself she wouldn't, of course, but she also knew herself, and she knew Claudia. Claudia had always been able to convince her that terrible ideas made some sort of sense. Perhaps that was the reason she had never judged her sister too harshly before. Maybe it was time, now, to put that behind her, to look at her sister in a truer light.

She loved Claudia, she did, but Claudia was not perfect. Dinah would stay by her side, of course, and do whatever she could to help Claudia find her way back to a more balanced path.

"You'll come to the market with me today, won't you?" Claudia asked around a bite of toast. "*Mamm* says she has too much on."

Dinah thought for a moment. She had her daily chores to do, and she needed to mend her apron, but that could just as easily be done tomorrow if she didn't have time today. It might be pleasant, she thought, to spend a little extra time with her sister on this errand. It was likely they needed some form of bonding after the events of the last week.

"All right," she said. "I'll get started on my chores now, and we can probably go in a few hours."

Two and a half hours later, she'd done everything she needed to do for the morning. It was amazing, she thought, what she could achieve in so little time when she really set her mind to it.

She and Claudia headed into town together, walking since *Dat* had taken the buggy to transport some building supplies to Jonathan's place an hour earlier. It was a long walk into town, past fields and hedgerows and winding streams. It was cold out, but there was no snow or frost on the ground to impede their journey, and the brisk pace they kept warmed them.

They reached the mercantile by late morning. Mostly, they only browsed, but Dinah felt it was as good a time as any to treat themselves to a tasty doughnut and a sweet-smelling soap each. Dinah also bought a new roll of white thread, unable to recall if she had enough for her apron.

Afterward, they browsed some of the other shop windows. Then, unable to stand the cold for so much longer, they headed into a second-hand bookshop. It was toasty warm inside, with small electric heaters against every wall. Dinah unfastened her cloak and pulled off her gloves, placing them beside Claudia's on the coat rack by the door.

They perused in silence for a while, occasionally watched by the store owner, an elderly man with small, round glasses perched low on his nose. Claudia hovered in the romance section, while Dinah headed straight for non-fiction, for histories of the town and wildlife guides.

She was flipping through a recently published book on native bird species when she sensed someone behind her.

"That's a good one," Aaron said, his voice low and soft. "There's a really good chapter on woodpeckers. You should get it."

Dinah turned, taking a small step back from him. He was standing very close, peering at what she was reading.

"Perhaps another time," she said. "Claudia tells me I have far too many bird books already, and I think maybe she's right."

"Nonsense. You can never have too many bird books. Claudia doesn't know what she's talking about," he said, his voice teasing.

"Are you talking about me?" Claudia's voice arched sharp from the other side of the shelf. "I might not know much about birdlife, but I certainly know a full bookshelf when I see one. She'll be overrun with the things if she's not careful."

Aaron laughed. "I didn't see you there," he admitted. "But of course, where one sister is, the other's likely not far away."

Dinah frowned at that. For one thing, it wasn't true, and she liked to think she had *some* independence from her sister, thank you very much.

"I'm afraid, Aaron Burner, that you don't know what you're talking about." Claudia's voice was amused, and she appeared around the side of the bookshelf a moment later. "But I'll forgive you, I suppose. Would you care to have lunch with us?"

"I can't, I'm afraid. I only have a spare ten minutes or so. But if you're looking for a lift home, I can offer you that. I didn't see your buggy outside."

"Such a gentleman," Claudia said, turning to Dinah. "Isn't he?"

Dinah turned back to the bookshelf and slotted the bird book back into its place.

"I couldn't say," she said. "Who can tell what he's hiding under such a placid mask."

When she turned around again, Aaron was looking at her, a puzzled sort of frown on his face. Dinah felt her cheeks heat up, and she hoped she hadn't turned pink. She had only meant those words teasingly. Unfortunately, she didn't have her sister's amused attitude, and it was all too likely she'd sounded scathing instead. *Don't make jokes*, Claudia had told her once. *Your delivery is terrible.*

"We'd love a ride home," Claudia said, breaking the awkward silence that had fallen around them. "It's so cold out."

"That's the end of January in Indiana for you," Aaron said.

Dinah loved the sound of his laugh. If only she had been the one to coax it out of him. But of course, it was Claudia. It had always been Claudia. Dinah sighed to herself and followed the two of them out into the street.

Chapter Eight

Aaron had trouble resisting the urge to sneak glances over his shoulder at Dinah on the ride home. He had felt, over the past few weeks, that they had been growing a little closer on their way to becoming good friends. But her comment at the bookstore had thrown him. Did she really think he was hiding something? And what? She had never been exactly warm toward him. Perhaps, she really didn't like him at all.

He tried to focus on the road ahead and to put thoughts of her aside, but it was hard when she was so close to him, sitting right behind him, her voice low as she chatted to her sister over the rumble of the buggy over the bumpy road. He could barely hear what she was saying, and that was fine. Claudia's voice was louder, but Aaron found it hard to listen. He was too lost in his own thoughts, and whatever this feeling was that was growing inside of him. He'd been sweet on girls before, even courted a couple for a spell, but none of them had been quite like Dinah.

In the past, what he had always felt for a girl seemed a little half-hearted. They'd been nice girls, kind enough and not bad looking, but there was something about Dinah, something he found hard to pinpoint. Her stoicism, perhaps. The way she held herself, back straight and chin raised. She spoke little, and when she did, it was always with a cool tone, but she wasn't unkind—quite the opposite in fact. But she was so hard to read.

Sometimes, he fancied she cared for him a little in return, a glance here or there or something in her tone of voice when she spoke to him, but it wasn't enough to really *know*. Perhaps, one day, he'd gather the courage to ask her, but certainly not today, and not likely even this week or this month. It was too likely that she'd disapprove of him for it, and he wasn't sure he could handle her rejection. Had she ever really paid him much attention at all? He didn't think so. Perhaps, he could change that, but it would take time, that was certain. No, best to wait and see for now, he thought.

He dropped the two sisters home and watched as they walked up the drive, side by side. Again, he wondered how two sisters who seemed so close could be so different from one another. His mother had often made comments about Claudia in the past, and he knew she'd thought the two of them might court one day, but he'd never felt that way about her. Not the way he felt about Dinah.

He turned the buggy around, and headed for home, trying to put all thoughts of Dinah Baer out of his head—at least for the time being.

Outside work had always been rather soothing to Aaron. He enjoyed being outdoors, even in the middle of the Indiana winter. He held a nail between his lips while he fumbled about the cold ground for the hammer he'd set down just a moment before. He didn't see Claudia approach, but when she called his name he turned, and immediately put down the hammer he'd just picked up. He took the nail from his mouth and set it on top of the fence post where he could find it again later, and stood, brushing dirt from the knees of his slacks.

"Claudia," he said, unable to hide his surprise. "To what do I owe the pleasure?"

Claudia smiled, but immediately he could tell it was not a happy smile. Tears sprang from her eyes, and she hurriedly wiped them away with a gloved hand. She sniffed. "I'm sorry. I just needed someone to talk to."

Aaron frowned. "Where's Dinah?"

Claudia shook her head. "I don't want to talk to her. I need to talk to someone who won't judge me. And Dinah, well, she tries her best to be kind, but I'm afraid she'll be angry with me. Oh, you'll probably be angry too, but you always hide it so well."

Aaron sighed and walked toward her. "Come on," he said. "Let's go and sit in the barn. It's always quiet in there. No one will bother us, and it's a whole lot warmer than out here."

Usually, Claudia would have made some tasteless joke about that, but today she only gave a weak smile and said, "Thank you."

Inside the barn, he sat her down and took a seat across from her, leaving a reasonable amount of space between them. "All right," he said, after a moment. "Tell me what's happened."

Claudia shook her head. "You'll hate me," she said, her voice thick with tears. "*I* hate me."

"Don't say that," Aaron said quickly. "Whatever it is you've done, *Gott* loves you. And He can't be wrong, can he?"

Claudia only sighed. "Everything's such a mess, Aaron. I really thought Gary was 'the one' for me, but now I realize how wrong I was. And now... Oh, Aaron. It's so awful. I just feel so ashamed."

Aaron leaned forward and took her hands in his. "Whatever it is, you can tell me. I won't judge you. I promise. Besides, what happened has been over for more than a month now."

She sniffed loudly, took a deep breath, and said, "I'm with child."

Aaron could only stare blankly at her, his mouth agape. Seconds seemed to stretch out into impossible minutes, as her reality broke open in his mind. Whatever his feelings about what Claudia had done, whatever desire he might have to tell her that yes, actions like that usually did have big consequences, Claudia was upset, and in need. He went to her side and put his arm around her. He held her for a moment while she cried, rubbing her back.

"Have you told your parents yet?"

Claudia shook her head. "*Ach,* how can I? I just can't."

"You have to," he told her. "You can't lie to them. Not again. They're going to find out anyway. And I think... I really think they'll forgive you, and they'll want to help. *I* want to help."

Claudia pulled back and blinked at him, her eyes still full of tears. "You do?"

"*Jah,* I really do. If there's anything I can do, just ask."

"I-I don't..." Claudia sniffed, and rubbed at her eyes. "*Nee,* it's too much to ask. I can't."

A deep sense of ill-boding filled him, then. His shoulders slumped, and already he knew what she was going to ask.

"The only way you can really help me," she said, "is if you marry me."

The next few days, Dinah threw herself into her chores. She had grown used to doing more than her share while Claudia was gone. Now that Claudia was back, it was hard to find enough to do. Claudia seemed to be working hard to impress their parents, to prove herself once again. Dinah should have been glad about that, but there was still a bitter seed lodged in her heart. Did Claudia really expect to fix things so easily or so quickly?

And it wasn't just that. Aaron was coming around more and more. Dinah might have been glad of that, once, but now it only made her feel alone and angry. She knew he was coming by to see Claudia, for he seemed to think Claudia needed him. As a friend, or something more, Dinah wasn't sure. She'd always thought Aaron rather admired Claudia, and it had been no big surprise to her when Claudia had told them all that dark lie—that she and Aaron were courting. It had made sense then, and it would make sense now, although Dinah hoped for Aaron's sake it wasn't true.

Or for her own sake, she wasn't really clear on that. Was she being selfish? Jealous, definitely, but that had always been her secret sin. Jealousy was nothing new to her. Anger was, though. She had never felt this way before, as though dark tendrils were creeping through her, around her chest and throat. Sometimes, she just wanted to run away.

Instead, she prayed. All she wanted was the best outcome for all of them, for whatever would help them all heal and move on, together, as a family. Church was a help, and Dinah threw herself into services and hymn sing, focusing more on the bishop's teachings than ever.

Claudia, though, seemed more distant in preaching service than she did even at home. Perhaps it was guilt eating away at her. Part of Dinah hoped it was that. Claudia *should* feel guilty.

It was a warm day for February when Claudia approached Dinah in the barn. Dinah had been taking a moment's rest after unloading the week's feed, enjoying some solitude, but she was not unhappy to see her sister. She had convinced herself days ago that despite all their difficulties, it was a joy to have her sister back around. She had, after all, come so close to losing her, albeit by Claudia's own will.

"I need to tell you something," Claudia said. Her teeth nibbled at her lower lip, the same way Dinah's did when she was concerned about something.

Dinah's heart froze. Was Claudia leaving again?

Claudia sat down on the bale of hay beside her and sighed. She wrapped her arms around herself and shivered.

Dinah waited in silence. She didn't want to force Claudia into speaking before she was ready.

"You won't like this," Claudia said.

Unable to bear it any longer, Dinah spoke. "Just tell me."

"I'm pregnant."

The world seemed to tilt, and the gloomy barn with its musty, straw smell seemed to recede for a moment. Had Dinah misheard? But no, of course, she hadn't.

"I told *Mamm* and *Dat* last night," Claudia said.

"That could not have gone well," Dinah said, trying to hold herself together.

"*Nee,* it did not. But they're not going to kick me out, so that's *gut* I suppose. Actually, they were quite practical about it. I already have a plan, anyway."

Dinah nodded. Practicality was the only thing for it. "So, what is this plan of yours? I'll help if I can, of course."

Her shock was ebbing now in the face of Claudia's rational tone, and all that remained was concern for her sister and the child growing inside of her. Whatever Dinah could do to protect them, she would.

Claudia sighed. "Aaron's agreed to marry me. I was so upset, I just spilled everything out to him, and he was so sweet, really. He told me he would help me any way he could, and really, that's the only way he can help me. He said he'd do it."

Dinah nearly choked. She couldn't speak, couldn't even *think*. For Claudia to mess up her own life was one thing, but to drag Aaron into it? To ask him to save her? He didn't need to. Dinah would help. And *Mamm* and *Dat*, or perhaps Claudia could find someone else to marry. There *had* to be someone else. It couldn't be Aaron. It just *couldn't*.

She jolted upright, then, and walked away. It was the only thing she could do to save them both from her wrath. She walked away without looking back. She wasn't sure where she was going, only that she had to go somewhere, *anywhere,* as far away from Claudia as she could get.

Aaron is going to marry my sister. The thought kept circling around in her head, clanging mercilessly, like it was somehow so much worse than the fact that Claudia was pregnant. Maybe it was. Dinah could forgive Claudia almost anything, but taking Aaron when she didn't even love him, just because it was convenient?

That, Dinah was not sure, she could ever forgive.

Chapter Nine

The following days after Claudia's admission, Aaron couldn't quite seem to catch hold of his thoughts. He wanted to help his friend, of course he did, but he also wished she had never told him, never asked him. But how could he refuse? He wanted a good life for Claudia and for her child, and how could she have that if he didn't help them? They would have no money, no community, nothing. Claudia would be gossiped about; her reputation ruined.

He felt as though there was a heavy weight strapped to his chest, and he was wading out into deep water.

It wouldn't be so bad, he tried to convince himself. He loved Claudia, in a way... He had always cared for her and enjoyed spending time with her. He wasn't *in love* with her, but he knew that wasn't always so important. They could make things work; he was sure.

But then there was Dinah. If he married Claudia, he would have to see Dinah marry someone else. He could never be with her, and he knew, deep in his heart, that it would be a regret he'd carry for a very long time.

But it was done. He'd told Claudia that yes, he would help her. He would marry her. He had to stand by that commitment now. His parents weren't so happy about the engagement when he told them. They knew nothing of Claudia's condition, but there had been rumors lately about Claudia's supposed trip to Illinois. But neither of his parents being big gossips, they put those rumors out of mind and eventually congratulated them both.

Aaron talked to the bishop after preaching service that Sunday. Aaron had a strange feeling while they were talking that he was floating, drifting away, and the room and the bishop were getting further and further away. Eventually, he came back to himself, and had to ask the bishop to repeat what he'd just said.

They would marry in mid-February, it was decided, just two weeks from now. He knew people would talk—no one ever married this early in the year—but Aaron couldn't control that. They didn't *know* anything, and he and Claudia would hold their heads high.

But ... February. Two weeks. It was really no time at all.

"I'm going to Illinois," Dinah declared over breakfast on Monday morning. The night before, Claudia had announced the date for her wedding. It was just two weeks away. Dinah had decided that she didn't want to be there for it. She didn't think she could bear it—seeing Claudia marry Aaron. Aaron, the man whom Dinah now knew, she had loved for so long.

Aaron, whom Claudia *didn't* love.

And the worst thing? Aaron probably loved Claudia. Because why else would he do something like this if he didn't love her? Which naturally meant that he didn't love Dinah. It was a cruel way for *Gott* to answer her questions. Perhaps it was for the best, and Dinah could eventually move on, but it didn't *feel* like it was the best. Not even a little.

"Why would you go to Illinois?" *Mamm* asked, frowning.

"I want to visit Judith," Dinah said, although it wasn't strictly the truth. She liked her cousin, Judith, and Judith's husband, Mark, but of course, that wasn't the reason she wanted to go *now*. "It's been a long time since I last saw her."

"Did you write her and ask?"

"I sent a letter this morning." Dinah would hopefully get a

reply in the next few days. She knew Judith wouldn't refuse her—they'd been close growing up, and it really *had* been a long time since they'd spent any time together. Years, in fact.

"Very well, then," her mother said, but she was frowning, and her tone was a little too sharp.

Three days later, Dinah had her reply. Of course, she could come and visit, although Judith was a little surprised at her haste. Dinah packed her bag as soon as she read the letter.

"I know you're not happy about your sister's marriage," *Mamm* said to her late that morning. "And neither am I. But it *is* happening, and you need to get on board. I won't have Claudia's reputation destroyed."

"I would never do that," Dinah said, angry that her mother would even think she might tell someone outside their family. "I won't even tell Judith the truth of things. I can promise you that. I just want to get away for a few days to enjoy my cousin."

Mamm nodded, her look more sympathetic now. "I wish I could do that, too," she said. "Get away for a while. But I don't have the luxury. You go and enjoy yourself, but don't stay too long. We'll need your help with the wedding."

Dinah nodded, but already she knew she wouldn't be coming home for the wedding—not if she could help it.

Dinah had hoped to sneak away to the bus without too much fuss the next morning, but Aaron had come by early. She was the only one around, her packed bag waiting in the front room. She hadn't bothered with breakfast, only with a warming lemon tea that she decanted into a flask for the journey to come.

Aaron stood in the expansive kitchen, his hands loose at his sides. He kept looking around the room, as if he were waiting for something or someone. Claudia, probably, although he hadn't asked for her.

"She'll be up soon," Dinah said, turning the cook stove down, but not off. "Have some tea if you like."

Aaron shook his head. "Actually," he said. "I'm here to talk to you."

Dinah raised her eyebrows. "Me?" she said. "What for?"

"Uhm, well... Can you sit down for a moment?" he asked, and Dinah sat.

Aaron took the seat opposite, his hands fidgeting together on the tabletop. When he said nothing, Dinah sighed. She felt like there was some huge gulf between them now, and she wished to bridge it. After all, he was going to be her brother-in-law.

"Look," she said. "I admire what you're doing. Helping my sister like this. It's very *gut* of you."

"But...?" Aaron asked.

Dinah hadn't meant there to be a 'but'. Aaron had heard something in her voice she'd thought she'd hidden.

"But," she continued, drawing the word out. "I just don't want her bad decisions to harm you. If you want to marry her, that's one thing, but if you don't..."

Aaron sighed. "I want to help her. I can't see her suffer, even if it is her own fault. But... I don't know, Dinah. You tell me. Do you think there's a *gut* reason why I shouldn't marry her?"

Dinah stared at him for a moment. This was it, she realized. She could tell him everything now. Tell him she loved him, that she always had. But what then? He might not feel the same way—he almost certainly didn't. He might not want to marry Claudia, but that didn't mean he would want to marry *her*.

She pressed down her anguish and shook her head. "I can't think of a reason," she said after a long moment. The words felt like they were choking her. "If you're looking for one, you need to come up with it yourself."

He hung his head then, staring down at his hands clasped together on the table. Dinah's heart ached for him. Claudia had put him in an awful situation, but then, he had agreed to it. If he didn't want to do it, that was his decision, but Dinah wasn't going to stop him.

If Aaron wanted her to give him a reason, he was out of luck.

She loved him, but if he had any feelings for her, he would have to figure them out himself. And if not, well, Dinah didn't want to be the one to lay it all out for him to trample over. Because if she told him the truth, and he *still* married Claudia? Well, she didn't think she could bear that.

Chapter Ten

Dinah thought she might find some peace at Judith's home in Land Creek, Illinois, but instead she merely felt alone. Judith and Mark were wonderful hosts, and Dinah had enjoyed seeing them again and playing with their two young sons, Abel and Jacob. But being away hadn't changed anything.

If anything, it only pointed out more sharply what she wanted for herself.

But at least, she thought, she didn't have to witness the mess back home. But still, she knew it was there. She wanted to pretend it wasn't happening, but she couldn't. It might have been easier if she had actually fought with Claudia, but instead she'd just walked away. Likely, Claudia had no idea how much she was hurting Dinah, but it was also likely that if she did, she wouldn't care. Claudia always did what was best for Claudia. She always had. And now she was using Aaron to do that, hurting him and hurting Dinah in the process.

But Dinah was used to it. She could take a little hurt. She was almost callous to it by now. But Aaron... What had he done to deserve this? Except being a kind and honorable person.

Dinah didn't want to think it, but she knew in her heart that Claudia had known Aaron wouldn't refuse to help a friend. She had played on his sympathies in order to get him to do what she wanted. She had used him before as an excuse, and that had been bad enough, but this was so, so much worse.

Dinah stood for a while on her cousin's porch without her cloak, letting the cold soak into her bones. It was slightly warmer here than it had been back home, but not by much. Winter still had the north of the country in a vice.

"Good morning, cousin." Judith's voice was soft behind her.

Dinah hadn't heard her open the door, but Judith's approach didn't startle her. She turned and smiled, although she didn't feel very much like smiling at all.

"Why are you standing out in the cold when there's a perfectly good heat stove to stand beside?"

"I like the cold," Dinah said.

"No, you don't," Judith told her, her voice kind. "Come inside. I'll make some tea and you can tell me about what's troubling you, if you want, or you can sit there in silence and contemplate your worries in the warmth."

Reluctantly, Dinah followed Judith back inside. It *was* nicer inside, she decided, as she took a seat at the kitchen table and clasped the cup of hot ginger tea Judith set in front of her.

"Would you like some toast and jam?" Judith offered.

Dinah shook her head. She hadn't been very hungry these last couple of weeks, usually only able to pick at meals. While it was nice of Judith to offer, she knew she wouldn't be able to manage more than a mouthful.

"Very well. But you must eat dinner later. I'm not having my beloved guest fainting on me because of low blood sugar."

"You're sounding like *Aenti* Cathy now," Dinah told her.

Judith chuckled. "You're horrible," she said. "I'm *nothing* like my *mamm*."

"Of course not," Dinah said, smirking.

"Be quiet."

"That's no way to speak to your beloved guest."

"The beloved part is lessening by the second," Judith bit back.

Dinah smiled and sipped her tea. For a moment, she had almost forgotten the turmoil back home. That was something, at least.

"Oh, I forgot. There was a letter for you yesterday. But then Abel tracked mud all through the house, and it completely slipped my mind."

Dinah didn't mind the delay. If there was a letter for her here, it could only be from her family. Probably Claudia. And Dinah was in no rush to hear from her right now.

Judith handed her the letter, and Dinah opened the envelope slowly, unfolded it, and drew in a breath before casting her eyes down the page.

She gritted her teeth. It was still happening. The wedding. There were three days left to go. And through the letter, she was being summoned to return home.

Aaron hadn't been able to get his thoughts in order for weeks, now. He stood, staring at the black suit hanging in the open door of his wardrobe. His wedding suit. It looked empty and lifeless hanging there like that. He sighed deeply. After Thursday, he'd be a married man. He would grow a beard.

The thought didn't excite him the way it should have. Instead, it felt like a sentence. Something final. It *was* final. But then, so was Dinah telling him she couldn't think of a reason he shouldn't marry her sister. She'd seemed so cool when she said those words, as though it didn't break his heart into pieces.

Now *that* was dramatic, he told himself. His heart wasn't

broken, merely bruised and aching. He could deal with that. He'd sprained his arm once and still managed to do most of his chores just fine. Well, with a fair amount of pain for a while, but the point was, he'd gotten through it. He'd adjusted. He'd kept going with his daily life despite the injury. This was a lot like that. It hurt now, but he knew the hurt would heal, and he had to keep on living his life.

Maybe his future wasn't what he'd expected, wasn't what he'd hoped for, but he could make it work. Not just for Claudia, but for the baby. A baby who would love him as though he were the father. He wanted that. He could be happy with that. And Claudia... Well, it wasn't a *terrible* match. They were friends, at least. They got along well. Some people settled for a lot less.

He didn't really want to go the Baer's house that afternoon, but Ella and John, Claudia's parents, had insisted he come around for dinner early. And tomorrow, they would all have dinner together, his family and Claudia's, to discuss... well, he wasn't sure what, but he supposed it was to get to know each other better, as family rather than just friends and neighbors.

Family. Dinah would be his sister-in-law. He pulled a face at the thought and tried to put it out of his mind.

As he walked up the driveway to the Baer's house, where Claudia would be waiting for him most likely, he thought briefly about just turning around and heading back the other way. He snorted to himself. Of course, he wouldn't do that. It was a terrible thought, something fleeting and fanciful and selfish. Maybe *that* was the reason Dinah didn't like him. Or one of the reasons, at least. Likely, she had noticed other flaws in him, too. He sighed and knocked on the door.

"You don't have to knock, you know," Claudia told him. She'd said this to him before, several times over the years, but of course he still knocked every time. It was only polite. "You'll certainly have to get out of this habit when we're married."

When they were married. Aaron held back another sigh. At first, they would live with Claudia's parents when they were married. Lately, Aaron had stood in his room several times, looking at his scant belongings, knowing it wouldn't take long to pack them, but also utterly unable to bring himself to do so.

"Are you coming in or not?" Claudia said, frowning. "I'm getting cold standing here."

He forced a smile then. "Of course, I'm coming in. Sorry. How are you?"

It had only been a day since he'd last asked her that. He couldn't help himself. It should have been getting annoying by now, but Claudia smiled. "I'm okay, thanks to you."

Something fluttered in Aaron's heart. There was that, at least. He needed Claudia to be all right, needed to protect her as best he could. He was doing a pretty fair job of that.

Claudia led him into the front room. He stopped in the

doorway, his heart clenching in his chest. Dinah was there, sitting straight-backed in the chair closest to the window, darning a *kapp*. She looked better, he thought, more rested. Her blue eyes were unshadowed; although, her mouth still held an unhappy downturn.

She glanced up at him, and her mouth narrowed into a thin line. Still, her voice was friendly enough when she spoke.

"Aaron," she said, her mouth curving into a thin smile that didn't reach her eyes. "How are you?"

He nodded to her. "I'm well, thank you. Busy, of course, but that's always a *gut* thing. How was your trip to Illinois? How's your cousin?"

"My trip was quite nice, actually. It was nice to be away for a little while. And it was pleasant to catch up with Judith. She's doing very well. Her boys seem so big now. The youngest was only just born when I last saw him, and he's nearly four now."

Aaron smiled at that. "They do grow fast," he said. "You have to watch them pretty close, I guess."

"I think I'll ban mine from growing," Claudia said. "Babies are so cute, I think I'd like to keep him that way for ever."

"Hmm," Dinah said. "*Gut* luck with that."

Aaron smiled to himself. It was good to see Dinah again, despite knowing she didn't return his feelings for her. It felt a little as though scabbed-over wounds were reopening, just at the sight of her, but he almost didn't mind. Seeing her face again was worth it. How had it taken him so long to realize how wonderful she was? Why, it had taken years of her hanging around the periphery of his life. She had been barely separable from Claudia, and yet they had so rarely interacted directly. He could still have that, he supposed.

Chapter Eleven

Dinah threw herself into the outdoor chores over the next couple of days. Anything that would get herself out of the house and away from the wedding plans. Except, as one of Claudia's *newehockers*, she could hardly escape entirely. There was baking to be done for the wedding, pressing capes and aprons to make sure they looked their best, and the cleaning of the house.

Claudia spent a lot of her time sewing her dress and the dresses for Dinah, Beth, and their cousins Joanna and Grace, who were also set to be her attendants at the wedding. The dresses were a sky blue—Claudia's slightly paler than the other four. It was a beautiful dress, Dinah thought, looking at it when it was almost finished. But Claudia didn't seem so enthusiastic about it.

"I'll be buried in this same dress," she said, a depressed note to her voice.

Dinah had always thought that tradition was a beautiful one. If *she* was marrying Aaron Burner, then the dress she wore on that day would absolutely be the one she would want to be buried in. It was a spiritual connection to him, a symbol of their love. But of course, Claudia didn't really love Aaron. Her dress was a lie, and she would sit through every church service in that lie, and yes, she would be buried wrapped in that lie, too.

"It is a beautiful dress," Dinah told her sister. "You should appreciate it."

Claudia only sighed and went back to her sewing.

Dinah wanted to holler at her, but there was no point in that, and besides, it wasn't right to be shouting at a pregnant woman. It might upset the baby. So instead, she turned and stalked out of the room, her shoulders stiff, and went to help her mother in the kitchen instead.

Dinah had been doing a lot of praying lately. Praying for forgiveness, praying for strength and patience. Praying that everything would work out all right for all of them, even Claudia. She was tired of it, and that night she only said her prayers perfunctorily, out of habit. She had no energy to give to them, anymore. She only wanted to sleep.

She changed into her nightgown and climbed into bed. She was almost asleep when a knock at the door pulled her back into wakefulness.

"Come in," she called, and the door opened.

"Dinah," her mother said, and there was something in the way she said it that Dinah didn't like. "Have you seen your sister?"

Dinah sat up and shook her head. "*Nee*, I haven't," she said, dread creeping through her. "What's going on?"

"Oh, well, I'm sure it's nothing... It's just that I haven't been able to find her all evening. In fact, I haven't seen her since supper."

Dinah wanted to bury her face in her hands and scream, but she didn't. Instead, she pushed back the quilts and got out of bed.

"You don't... know anything, do you?" *Mamm* said, a slight accusatory note in her voice.

Dinah frowned. "*Nee*, not this time, *Mamm*," she said firmly. "If I did, I'd tell you, I promise."

"Maybe she just went for a walk. Brides often do get terribly nervous."

"Maybe," Dinah said. "But..." She thought of Claudia's

comment about the dress and how melancholy she'd sounded. "I don't think she's gone for a walk."

How like Claudia it would be, she thought, to run off the night before her wedding. Claudia had always thrived on drama. And what could be more dramatic than this?

Poor Aaron, Dinah thought. How would he feel, if that's what Claudia had done? Jilted. All those invitations given out, all the expectation from friends and family, some of them, like Judith and Mark, traveling long distances to be there for the wedding, and now... Would they have to call the whole thing off?

Her heart twisted. Had Claudia really left them again? How could she do that to them, after last time? Part of her hoped *Mamm* was right. Maybe Claudia *had* grown nervous and gone for a long walk to calm herself. She might come back soon enough.

But Claudia didn't come back. After a sleepless night, Dinah learned that she still hadn't returned, and she watched as the men headed out at first light to search for her. As for Dinah, she was tasked with telling Aaron.

That wasn't a job she wanted, not at all. She didn't think she could bear to tell him that Claudia had mostly likely left him, and that she might not come back. She didn't want to see the hurt in his eyes. She knew that pain only too well.

She walked slowly through the light sprinkling of snow that

had fallen in the night, as though delaying things would make them any easier. It was still half dark out, but she knew the way well enough, and it wasn't far.

It was Beth who answered the door; she was a sweet girl, barely fourteen, with all the energy and devotion of a puppy. She immediately saw something was wrong, but Dinah couldn't tell her before she told Aaron. Yet Beth wasn't stupid.

"Is it about the wedding?" she asked.

Dinah nodded.

"Claudia's called it off, *ain't so?*"

Dinah sighed. "I need to talk to Aaron," she said.

Beth nodded, and led her into the kitchen to wait while she fetched Aaron from his room.

When he arrived, he looked tired, like he hadn't slept well at all. Dinah could sympathize.

"You're here early," he said, and his voice sounded rough, like he was getting sick.

"Aaron," she started, unsure of how exactly she was going to say this. Best be honest and quick about it, she supposed. "I don't know how to tell you, but ... Claudia has disappeared again. She wasn't in her room last night, and she hasn't shown up this morning. I mean, she still might, but..."

"...but it's unlikely," he finished for her. "Well then, I suppose we better cancel the wedding."

"You don't sound very upset," Dinah said, frowning. She'd expected him to show a little reaction, at least.

"I... Well, I'm not," Aaron said with half a sigh. "Not really. I was marrying Claudia to help her, you know that. I'm just... disappointed she never said anything to me before taking off. Although, I shouldn't be surprised, now, should I?"

Dinah bit her lip. "I don't think Claudia was thinking about anyone other than herself," she admitted. "I suppose it's nothing personal. I'm sorry, Aaron. It's just... *her*. She'll be your best friend one minute, but she'll forget all about you the next minute when something better comes along."

"Something better..." Aaron said slowly. "This 'Gary' fellow, you mean?"

Dinah sighed. She hadn't meant to hurt his feelings. "Maybe," she said. "But my sister's a fool if she thinks there's a better man than... I mean, she's acting foolish. We all know that Gary's already left her once. If she's run back to him, the same thing will probably happen again."

"Do you think she'll come back here again, if that happens?"

Dinah shrugged. "It's possible. But I don't know if she'll be welcome back a second time."

"We're talking as though she's definitely gone," he said. "We don't know for sure and for certain, I suppose?"

Dinah shook her head. They didn't know for certain, but it was the most likely scenario, and she knew her sister.

"I hope she hasn't run off again," she murmured. "But right now... I don't think I'll see her again. At least, not for a long, long while."

Aaron sighed. "I'll pray for her." Dinah's heart lifted just a little at that. Aaron continued, "I wanted to help her, but I suppose only *Gott* can do that now."

Dinah nodded. "Only *Gott* can do that now."

"I won't lie to you, Dinah. I was having doubts. I hate to admit it because I'm the one who agreed to marry her. But... Well, I'm glad the wedding's off. I mean, I'd rather Claudia hadn't run away, but I don't think I was wise in agreeing to this."

"You don't?" Dinah said, her heart jumping a little in her chest.

Aaron sighed, his hands twitching on the table. After a moment, he reached across the wooden surface and grabbed Dinah's hand in his. Dinah's mouth dropped open, but she quickly closed it again. The feeling of his warm, rough hand over hers was divine.

"I don't love Claudia. Not that way, at least. And I asked you, once, if you thought I should marry her. You didn't tell me not to, and I have no right to think I might have a chance with you, but ... I *want* a chance with you." He shifted in his seat. "The wedding is off, and that means I'm free from my promise to your sister, so ... Dinah Baer, would you allow me to court you? This is horrible timing, and well... if you agree, perhaps we should wait a while, but I want you to know my intentions. I should have spoken well before this. I should have made my feelings clear."

Dinah's face split into a shocked grin. She placed her other hand over Aaron's and gripped firmly. "I... I..." She was so overcome, she couldn't continue.

He smiled at her. "Like I said, this is horrid timing. I understand if you turn me down. But *ach*, Dinah, I hope you won't."

She blinked and tried to swallow. "And this is the truth? You're telling me the truth."

He chuckled warmly and squeezed her hand. "I'm telling you the truth."

"Then, *jah*. *Jah*, I want you to court me," she told him, her heart swelling to huge proportions. "You're the most wonderful man I've ever met. Sorry, that's...that's a bit forward, but... *Ach*, I've always thought it."

Aaron laughed then, a throaty chuckle. "You have? Sometimes, I thought perhaps you disliked me."

"*Disliked* you?" Dinah was shocked. "Not in the slightest."

Aaron's grin faded into a gentle smile. "I'm so glad to hear it."

They sat there together for a moment longer, enjoying the quiet and each other's company. Eventually, they released each other's hands and scraped their chairs back.

There was a wedding to cancel.

Epilogue

One Year Later

Dinah stood in the kitchen, watching the morning sky fade from pitch black to navy blue as she made the morning tea and began to prepare breakfast for her family. She turned the letter she held over in her hands. It had arrived two days ago, but she hadn't been able to bring herself to open it yet, too afraid of what its contents might reveal.

The script on the envelope was familiar, and it had brought a wave of nostalgia and grief crashing through her. Now that wave had faded to a gentle lapping, ever present but not so overwhelming. She took a deep breath and opened the letter.

Dearest Sister,

I know perhaps you won't want to hear from me, but I just keep thinking of how it's your birthday next month, and between that and Christmas just passed... Well, I miss you.

Maybe you've been worried about me, and I'm sorry for that. I'm sorry I hurt you all. But I had to take my chance, you see. Gary, well, he realized he'd made a terrible mistake. He told me that when I left everything for him, he got scared—I'd made it too real, too quickly. I didn't really understand what he meant right then, but I was just so happy he'd come back to me. And I thought my boppli deserved to know her real father. And me... Well, I couldn't pass up the chance for true love. Would you?

Well, jah, perhaps you would. You're far too perfect for your own gut.

As for my daughter... My boppli is a girl, you know... She's a very happy, healthy child. We named her Evelynn. I wish you could meet her. I always imagined we'd sort of parent our kinner together, be there for each other. I suppose that will never happen now. I know I'm not welcome at home. If I come, I'll be shunned.

But I want you to know you are welcome in my home (see address above). I won't hold out hope that you'll visit, I just wanted to make sure you knew that I still love you, and even if you don't think of me as family anymore, you will always be my sister.

All my love,

Claudia

. . .

Dinah bit her lip, scanning the letter over again. Tears sprang from her eyes, and she let them fall. She sniffed loudly and choked back a sob.

"Dinah?" Aaron's voice came from the doorway. "Is something wrong?"

She turned to face him, not wanting to hide her tears from him. She shook her head and handed him the letter. She watched as he read it, his hands shaking a little as he did so. Then, he folded the letter neatly, and handed it back.

"It sounds to me," he said, a smile spreading across his face, "as though Claudia's all right, after all."

"I have a niece," Dinah said. She'd often wondered over the past year about Claudia and her baby—what the baby was like, if Claudia was happy, if everything was all right with them. She was sad that the baby would never know them, would never grow up in the love of the church, but she was glad to hear they were otherwise well, at least. "Or, sort of a niece. I suppose not really, now that we've cut all ties with Claudia, but—"

"Just because the district has shunned Claudia, doesn't mean you have to stop thinking of her as your sister. I'll bet you parents still think of her as their daughter, even if they never say so."

Dinah nodded. He was right, of course. She knew she would never visit Claudia's home, would most likely never even write back to her, but she also knew that Claudia would always be her sister, despite what had happened.

She put her arms around Aaron, then, glad he was there. "I do love you," she told him.

"I certainly hope so," he said. "We are married, after all."

She laughed lightly at that and held him all the tighter.

The End.

Continue Reading...

Thank you for reading **Her Sister's Lie! Are you wondering what to read next?** Why not read **Smitten at Christmas? Here's a peek for you:**

Sunlight filtered in through the gap in the curtains of Rebecca's small, undecorated room. She opened her eyes and sat bolt upright. She had overslept. She swung her legs out of bed and into her slippers and hurried, still in her nightdress, down the hall and into Esther's room. The old woman set down the book she'd been reading and glowered at her.

"What time do you call this?" she snapped. "I've been lying here for hours."

Rebecca doubted Esther had been awake any longer than forty minutes or so, but she didn't argue. Instead, she helped Esther out of bed, massaging feeling back into the woman's cold feet before helping her stand. Esther then shrugged out of Rebecca's grip and made her own, slow way to the bathroom.

After toileting, Rebecca helped Esther wash and then dressed her. The old woman's fingers were swollen and bent, and she struggled to lift her arms over her head. Dressing her was slow, but they had long since gotten into a rhythm that meant it didn't take as long as it used to.

At first, Esther had resisted much of Rebecca's help, despite paying her for it. Now, she accepted the daily routine they had gotten into, more or less. Occasionally, she still snapped at Rebecca for being too rough or not fastening her *kapp* exactly right. Today though, there was more grumbling than usual.

"Silly girl," Esther snapped. "This apron has a smudge on it. Find me another and wash this one."

Rebecca bit back a frustrated sigh and did as she was told. She knew Esther's bad mood was her own fault for sleeping in. Usually, her internal clock was far more reliable than any other, and she never set the alarm on the little wind up clock her father had given her one Christmas. Today, however...

Today was off to a bad start. She just had to hope it would get better.

It didn't. After washing Esther's clothes and hanging them out to dry on the lines in the basement, Esther demanded she weed the barren front flowerbed, despite the dark clouds threatening rain. Isaac Farmer usually did the beds, but he was in his sixties himself and had come down with the flu last week. Not to mention, who weeded flowerbeds in the late fall? It was absurd, but Rebecca had learned long ago not to argue with the woman.

After coming back inside, she made Esther a cup of nettle tea, helped her to the toilet, and made them both a quick lunch. Esther was content to sit with her darning for a while, only occasionally complaining about the arthritis in her fingers. It was a warm day, not very cold for late November, and the fire was going in the warming stove. Esther's arthritis was more or less leaving her alone today, which was a blessing for them both.

VISIT HERE To Read More:

http://www.ticahousepublishing.com/amish-miller.html

Thank you for Reading

If you **love Amish Romance, Visit Here:**

https://amish.subscribemenow.com/

to find out about all **New Hannah Miller Amish Romance Releases! We will let you know as soon as they become available!**

If you enjoyed ***Her Sister's Lie,*** would you kindly take a couple minutes to leave a positive review on Amazon? It only takes a moment, and positive reviews truly make a difference. I would be so grateful! Thank you!

Turn the page to discover more Hannah Miller Amish Romances just for you!

More Amish Romance from Hannah Miller

Click HERE for Hannah Miller's Amish Romance

https://ticahousepublishing.com/amish-miller.html

About the Author

Hannah Miller has been writing Amish Romance for the past seven years. Long intrigued by the Amish way of life, Hannah has traveled the United States, visiting different Amish communities. She treasures her Amish friends and enjoys visiting with them. Hannah makes her home in Indiana, along with her husband, Robert. Together, they have three children and seven grandchildren. Hannah loves to ride bikes in the sunshine. And if it's warm enough for a picnic, you'll find her under the nearest tree!

Made in the USA
Coppell, TX
15 May 2021